ILLUSTRATED CLASSICS

THE SECRET GARDEN

FRANCES HODGSON BURNETT

ABRIDGED BY ANNE ROONEY · ILLUSTRATED BY BRUNO MERZ

Sandy Creek
NEW YORK

Death in India

Mary Lennox was a skinny, plain little girl who always frowned unpleasantly. Her hair was thin and pale, and her face was rather pale, too, because she was always sick and stayed indoors. Mary lived in India with her mother and father, but her father was always busy and her mother had never really wanted her. She was looked after by servants. Everyone did whatever Mary wanted, and she became very selfish and spoiled.

One hot morning, when Mary was nine years old, her own servant, Saidie, didn't come to dress her as usual. Mary had a tantrum, but no one would tell her what was going on.

When she was tired of being angry, Mary wandered outside and made a pretend garden by sticking red flowers into the soil. She overheard her mother talking with a young army officer. Her mother was beautiful and wore pretty lace dresses and Mary loved looking at her. But this morning her mother looked scared.

"Is it so very bad?" Mary heard her say to the officer.

"Awful," he answered.

Mary listened as the officer explained that a disease called cholera had broken out.

Just then, a terrible wail came from the servants' quarters, and Mary's mother clutched the man's arm.

"I am afraid someone has died," whispered the officer.

Mary soon learned that it was her servant, Saidie, who had become sick in the night. Awful things happened quickly after that and more servants died.

Mary hid in her nursery all of the next day, but no one came to look for her. It seemed she was entirely forgotten. The house grew quiet and Mary slept for a long time.

When she woke, a man she had never seen before opened the door. He was horrified to see her, but Mary was only angry.

"I am Mary Lennox. I fell asleep when everyone had the cholera. Why was I forgotten?" she said, stamping her foot.

"Poor little thing!" he said. "There's nobody left."

And so Mary discovered that both her father and mother had died. Mary didn't know her parents well enough to miss them, and she was far too selfish to be sad about it.

Mary lived with a vicar's family until she could be sent back to England. The vicar had five children, who argued all the time. Mary didn't like them. On her second day, she was making another garden when one of the boys suggested she plant some flowers among the rocks. Mary shouted at him and he began to tease her.

"Mistress Mary, quite contrary! How does your garden grow?" he sang.

Soon all the children called her "Mistress Mary" and Mary hated it. She was relieved when the news came that she was to move to England and live with her uncle, Mr. Archibald Craven, at Misselthwaite Manor.

Misselthwaite Manor

Mary traveled by ship to England. It was a long and difficult journey. The officer's wife who had been asked to look after Mary on the ship was glad to hand her over to Mr. Craven's housekeeper in London.

Mrs. Medlock, the housekeeper, was plump with red cheeks and black, beady eyes. Mary thought she looked unpleasant. Mrs. Medlock thought Mary looked spoiled.

They took a long train journey. Mary sat silently until, eventually, Mrs. Medlock said, "You're going to a strange place, lass. It's a big, gloomy house that's six hundred years old and has nearly a hundred rooms. It's right on the edge of the moor. Mr. Craven won't take any notice of you. He sees no one. He has a crooked back, and that set him off on the wrong foot. Until he married he was a bitter, miserable young man. His wife was a sweet, pretty young thing and changed him. But now she's dead, he doesn't care about anybody."

Mary was not concerned. She sat angrily while the rain poured down the windowpanes. She soon fell asleep and, when the train stopped, Mrs. Medlock shook her awake. A carriage took them across the moor to Misselthwaite.

Mary looked out of the window, curious, at last, to see where they were going.

She felt the long drive would never end.

"I don't like this place at all," she grumbled.

Finally, they stopped in front of a long, low house built around a stone courtyard.

Mrs. Medlock led Mary through a maze of staircases and corridors to her room. There was a fire in the fireplace and a meal on the table.

"Well, here you are! This room and the one next door are yours," Mrs. Medlock said. "You are to stay in them. Don't you forget that!"

In the morning, Mary opened her eyes to see a young housemaid cleaning the fireplace. The housemaid was called Martha. She saw Mary looking out of the window at the expanse of dull, purplish land that stretched into the distance.

"That's the moor," said Martha. "Do you like it?"

"No," said Mary. "I hate it. Who is going to dress me?"

"Can't you dress yourself?" Martha asked.

"No," replied Mary. "My servants always dressed me."

"Well, it's time you learned," said Martha. But, just this time, Martha did help Mary put on the new clothes that Mr. Craven had told Mrs. Medlock to buy. They were much nicer than the clothes she had worn to travel back from India.

At first, Mary ignored Martha as she chatted. In India, she had grown up in a house where servants were ignored, and she wasn't interested in what a maid had to say. But Mary soon began to listen as Martha talked about her home, her eleven brothers and sisters and how they all played on the moor. She especially liked to hear about Dickon, who had a pony of his own that he had found on the moor. But Mary did not admit this.

A Mystery

The next day, at breakfast, Mary did not feel like eating her porridge. Martha hated to see food wasted.

"My brothers and sisters have never had full stomachs in their lives. They're as hungry as young hawks," she said.

"I don't know what it is to be hungry," said Mary.

"Well, it would do you good to try it," Martha said. "Put on your coat and go and play outside."

"I don't want to," said Mary.

"Go on, now," Martha said. "Our Dickon goes off on the moor by himself for hours."

As there was nothing else to do, Mary did go outside after all. Before she went, Martha told her a story about a garden that no one had been in for ten years.

"Mr. Craven shut it when his wife died. It was her garden. He locked the door and buried the key," Martha said.

As Mary walked, she thought about the garden. She wondered whether she would be able to find it. She followed paths and walked through walled gardens until she saw an old man digging.

"What's through that door?" Mary asked him.

"A kitchen garden," he answered. "There are more beyond this one and an orchard, too."

Once in the orchard, Mary could see treetops peeping over a wall, and a bird with a bright red breast perched in one of them. The wall carried on past the orchard and Mary wondered if it was the wall of the secret garden.

Mary thought about the key to the garden. Why had Mr. Craven buried it? If he loved his wife so much, why did he hate her garden? For a long time she looked for a door, but couldn't find one. At last she walked back to the gardener and told him about the pretty bird she'd seen.

The man whistled and the bird landed near his foot.

"What kind of a bird is he?" Mary asked.

"He's a robin redbreast. Are you the lass from India?"

"Yes," Mary nodded. "What is your name?"

"Ben Weatherstaff," he answered with a rough chuckle, "and this little bird is the only friend I've got."

"I have no friends at all," said Mary.

"You're a good bit like me, then," Ben said. "Neither of us is very pretty and we're both as sour as we look."

Suddenly a clear, bright sound filled the air. The robin had flown to a tree near Mary and burst into cheerful song.

"He wants to be friends with you!" Ben said.

"Would you be friends with me?" Mary asked the robin.

"You sound like Dickon talking to his wild creatures."

"I've heard all about Dickon," said Mary.

The robin ended his song, gave a little shake of his wings, spread them, and flew away over the wall.

"He's flown into the garden with no door!" Mary cried.

"He lives there," said Ben. "Among the old rose trees."

"I should like to see the rose trees," said Mary. "There must be a door somewhere."

"None that anyone can find. Don't poke your nose in where it's not wanted. Now run along," Ben snapped.

The Garden without a Door

Every day seemed the same to Mary. Each morning she ate a little breakfast and then realized that if she didn't go out she'd have to stay in and do nothing —so she went out. Little did she know, this was the best thing she could have done. The fresh air was good for her and it soon put color in her cheeks and a sparkle in her eye. After a few days, she was hungry enough to eat all of her breakfast, and that pleased Martha.

Mary still hoped to find the door to the deserted garden. One day, she was looking up at a sprig of ivy hanging down from the wall when she saw the robin again. He twittered and hopped along, and Mary ran after him. Poor, thin, plain Mary actually looked pretty as she played. At last the robin flew to the top of a tree on the other side of the wall.

"He lives in the garden without a door," Mary said to herself. "How I wish I could see what it's like!"

The hidden garden gave her something to think about. At last, she felt pleased to have come to Misselthwaite. In India, she had always been too hot and never cared about anything. Now, she stayed outdoors all day, and when she sat down for her supper she felt hungry and healthy. She was no longer angry when Martha chattered away, and even quite liked to hear her talk.

A Cry in the Wind

One evening, Mary asked Martha why Mr. Craven hated the garden.

"There was an old tree with a branch like a seat," said Martha. "Mrs. Craven used to sit there. But, one day, the branch broke and she fell and died. The doctors thought Mr. Craven might go out of his mind."

Mary looked into the fire and listened to the wind. But she began to hear something else.

"Do you hear anyone crying?" she asked Martha.

"No," Martha answered. "It's the wind. Sometimes it sounds as if someone is lost on the moor, wailing."

"But listen," said Mary. "It sounds like it's coming from the house."

"It's the wind," Martha repeated firmly.

The next day it poured with rain, and Mary couldn't go out. She wandered around the house, exploring rooms she had never been in. On her way back to her own floor, she heard the crying again.

Mary put her hand on a tapestry next to her and, to her surprise, a door hidden behind it fell open. Mary peered through the door and saw Mrs. Medlock marching angrily along a corridor toward her.

"I heard crying," said Mary.

"You did not hear crying," Mrs. Medlock said, and she grabbed Mary and dragged her back to her room.

Mary sat on the rug, trembling with rage.

"There *was* someone crying!" she said to herself.

The Buried Key

Two days later, the sky was a startling blue and Mary could go outside again. Spring was coming. She looked at the green shoots of crocuses and daffodils coming up through the grass, and then she saw the robin pecking in a pile of freshly dug soil. There was something partly buried in the earth that looked like a ring. The robin flew away and Mary stooped to have a look and brushed away the soil. It was a large key!

"Perhaps it's been buried for ten years," she whispered. "Perhaps it's the key to the garden!"

Mary looked at the key for a long time. She was curious and desperately wanted to see what was inside the garden and what had happened to the old rose trees. She put the key in her pocket, so that if she *did* ever find the hidden door she would be ready.

While Mary was outdoors, Martha went to visit her mother. When she got back, she said she had shared news of Mary with her mother, brothers, and sisters. They were all eager to hear more and Mary promised to tell Martha new stories about India. Martha gave Mary a present from her mother.

"What is it?" Mary asked in wonder.

"It's a jump rope!" cried Martha.

"So, you have elephants and tigers and camels in India, but no jump ropes?"

Martha had to show Mary what to do, but she jumped rope until her cheeks were red.

Mary's Garden

As she jumped rope in the garden, Mary felt the heavy key in her pocket. When she saw the robin, she said, "Robin, yesterday you showed me the key. Now show me the door!"

What happened next seemed like magic. No sooner had she finished speaking than a gust of wind blew the hanging ivy aside and, for just a moment, Mary glimpsed a doorknob. She quickly pushed the ivy away, and there, right in front of her eyes, was the hidden door! She took the key from her pocket and turned it in the lock. The old door creaked as Mary pushed it slowly open and she took a few cautious steps forward. At last she had found it! At last she was standing inside the secret garden.

A thick tangle of climbing roses covered the high walls, but only their leafless stems remained. The roses had grown over the other trees, and hung in curtains and made bridges between them. Mary wondered if they were dead, but she didn't know enough about plants to tell. But the pale green shoots of growing plants pushed through the grass, so Mary knew that the garden was not completely dead. The grass under her feet was so thick that there didn't seem to be room for the shoots to grow. Mary dug away the weeds and grass around the new stalks with a piece of wood. She worked carefully and for a long time, until it was time to go in for lunch.

At the manor, Martha served Mary a lunch of meat and rice pudding, which Mary ate hungrily.

"I wish I had a little shovel," Mary said to Martha after she had eaten. "Then I could dig and make a garden of my own."

There was a little store in the village that sold garden tools and seeds. Martha suggested Mary should write to Dickon and ask him to buy them and bring them over. Mary had enough money because Mr. Craven left some for her each week. She was excited about the new shovel, but even more excited that she might meet Dickon.

The sun shone for a week, and every day Mary went back to work in the secret garden, digging and pulling up weeds with her hands and a piece of wood. Then, one day, on her way to the garden, she saw a boy standing under a tree playing a wooden pipe. He was about twelve years old and had a turned-up nose and rosy red cheeks. A squirrel clung to the trunk of the tree, and two rabbits sat nearby. She knew at once it had to be Dickon!

Dickon had brought the tools and some seeds for Mary, and offered to plant them. But, when Dickon asked where her garden was, Mary didn't know what to say.

"Can you keep a secret?" she said, clutching at his sleeve. "I've stolen a garden. Nobody wants it, or cares for it though. And no one ever goes there."

Meeting Mr. Craven

"Where is this garden?" asked Dickon.

Mary took him to the door, lifted the hanging ivy and led him into the secret garden. For two or three minutes, Dickon just stood and stared.

"I never thought I'd see this place," he said at last.

"Did you know about it?" asked Mary.

Dickon nodded. Mary asked Dickon if he thought the roses were all dead, but he cut a stem open to show her that they were still alive inside. Dickon saw the patches Mary had cleared around the bulbs.

"There's a lot of work to do here!" he said.

"Will you come again and help me to do it?" asked Mary. "Oh, do come, Dickon!"

"I'll come every day if you want me to," he answered.

They worked happily together, until the big clock struck the hour for lunch and Mary had to go inside.

Mary ate lunch quickly, eager to get back to Dickon, but then Martha said Mr. Craven had returned from London and wanted to see her. Mrs. Medlock led her to a room she had never seen before. Mr. Craven was sitting in an armchair by the fire. He had high, crooked shoulders and looked awkwardly at Mary.

"Are you well, child? Is there anything you want?" he asked.

"May I have a patch of ground to plant seeds?"

"You can have as much of the ground as you want," he sighed. "Take it and make things grow. Now please go, as I am tired."

Finding Colin

That night, Mary was woken by wind and rain beating against her window. She lay and listened and soon realized it wasn't just the wind she could hear—she could hear the crying sound again, too. Mary took a candle and padded to the corridor she had found behind the tapestry. The crying led her into a big room, where a boy lay sobbing in bed. Mary crept toward him

"Are you a ghost?" he sniffled when he saw Mary.

"No," she answered. "Are you?"

"No, I am Colin Craven. Who are you?"

"I am Mary Lennox. Mr. Craven is my uncle."

"He's my father," said the boy.

"Your father!" Mary gasped. "He has a child!"

Colin explained that he hated to be looked at, and that he was always sick.

"If I live, I may grow lumps on my back and be a hunchback, but I shan't live," he said. "My mother died soon after I was born and I make my father miserable."

"He hates the garden because she died," Mary said to herself.

"What garden?" Colin asked.

"Oh, just … just a garden she used to like," Mary stammered. She quickly changed the subject and told Colin all about her voyage from India. Colin told Mary how everyone had to do as he said, because being sick made him angry.

26

"How old are you?" Colin asked her.

"I'm ten," she answered, "and so are you, because when you were born the garden door was locked and the key was buried. And it has been locked for ten years."

"What garden door was locked? Where was the key buried? Who buried it?" asked Colin.

"Mr. Craven," said Mary, nervously. "He locked the door and buried the key. But I found it."

Colin kept asking questions.

"I'll make the servants take me to the garden!" he said.

"Don't do that!" Mary cried. "If you don't tell anyone I promise I'll find a way for us to go there together."

Once Colin agreed to her plan, Mary relaxed a little.

Martha was alarmed when Mary told her that she had found Colin, and then astonished that Colin had been willing to talk to her. Soon afterward, Colin even sent for Mary. Mary told him all about Dickon—how he was a friend of the animals and how they trusted him. When Colin started to talk about dying, Mary insisted that they talk about other things.

The two children soon realized that they were cousins and were laughing when Colin's doctor and Mrs. Medlock suddenly walked in. The doctor was worried that Mary made Colin too excited. But Colin said that Mary made him feel better and he would continue to see her. The doctor agreed, but warned Colin not to forget that he was very sick.

An Argument

For a whole week after that it rained, and Mary spent hours every day talking to Colin. But, on the first morning when the sky was blue again, she ran straight to the secret garden. Dickon was already digging and working hard when she arrived. Mary was thrilled to meet his fox cub, Captain, and a crow called Soot. She was excited, too, to tell him about Colin.

"If he was out here with us, he wouldn't be watching and waiting for lumps to grow on his back, and he'd be healthier," said Dickon. "It'd be good for him."

But, when Mary went to see Colin later on, he was furious with her.

"Why didn't you come to see me earlier?" he demanded.

"I was working in the garden with Dickon," answered Mary.

"I won't let that boy come here if you spend time with him instead of me!" he said.

"If you send Dickon away, I'll never come to visit you again," Mary shouted. "You're so selfish!"

"I'm not as selfish as you," snapped Colin, "because I'm always sick, and I'm sure there is a lump growing on my back, and I'm going to die."

"You're not going to die!" shouted Mary. "You just want people to feel sorry for you."

"Get out of my room!" shouted Colin, in a rage.

"I'm going," cried Mary. "And I won't come back!"

Animals in the Bedroom

That night, Mary was woken by terrible screaming and crying. She put her hands over her ears.

"Somebody ought to make him stop!" she shouted.

But just then, the nurse rushed in and begged her to go to Colin's room. Mary ran along the corridor.

"Just stop!" she shouted at Colin. "I hate you! Everybody hates you!"

"I can't stop!" he gasped.

"Yes, you can!" shouted Mary. "All that's wrong with you is a terrible temper!"

"I felt the lump," cried Colin. "I will have a hunch on my back and I will die."

"You didn't feel a lump!" Mary snapped. "There's nothing at all the matter with your back. Let me see!"

Mary looked at his spine and ran her hand down it.

"There's not a single lump there except for your backbones!" she said.

Colin breathed a sigh of relief. No one had ever spoken so angrily to him before, but neither had anyone ever reassured him like that.

"Do you think I'll grow up?" he asked his nurse.

"You probably will," she answered, "if you do not get into such a temper, do as you are told, and go out into the fresh air as much as you can."

"I would like to go there with you, Mary," said Colin, at last, "if Dickon will come and push my chair. I do so want to see Dickon and the fox and the crow."

The next day, Mary and Dickon made a plan. Mary ran to Colin's room while Dickon waited.

"It's so beautiful outside!" Mary said. "Spring has arrived! There are buds everywhere." She threw open the window to let in the fresh air and told Colin that Dickon was coming to visit him with his animals.

Colin couldn't wait to meet Dickon and the animals and told his nurse to bring them straight to his room.

"A boy and a fox and a crow and two squirrels and a newborn lamb are coming to see me this morning. I want them brought upstairs," he said.

The nurse gave a gasp and covered it up with a cough.

"Yes, sir," she answered.

"I'll tell you what you can do," added Colin, waving his hand. "You can tell Martha to bring them here. The boy is Martha's brother. His name is Dickon!"

Dickon came in smiling with the newborn lamb in his arms, the fox cub trotting by his side, a crow on his shoulder, and two squirrels. Colin couldn't believe his eyes. Dickon put the lamb on Colin's lap, pulled a bottle from his pocket and fed the lamb while answering all of Colin's questions. The three of them looked at pictures of flowers in a book that Mr. Craven had sent to Mary.

"I'm going to see all these flowers!" cried Colin, and together they planned a visit to the garden.

The Secret Uncovered

It wasn't long before Dickon pushed Colin's wheelchair to the ivy-covered walls around the secret garden.

"I used to walk here and think about finding the garden," said Mary. "And that is where I found the key. And here is the door! Dickon, push him in quickly!"

Little green leaves had crept over the walls and trees, and the grass was splashed with the gold and purple of crocuses. As the warm sun shone on Colin's face, he cried out, "I shall get well! And I shall live forever and ever!"

Colin watched as Mary and Dickon worked in the garden. They brought him things to look at: buds, a woodpecker's feather, the empty shell of a newly hatched bird. The afternoon was packed with new things, and the sun shone golden and warm on them.

"I never want this afternoon to end," Colin said, "but I'll come back tomorrow, and the day after. I will see everything grow here, and I'll grow here myself!"

But suddenly Colin stopped.

"Who's that man?" he whispered in alarm.

Mary and Dickon looked around to see Ben Weatherstaff glaring over the wall at them from a ladder. He shook his fist at Mary and shouted at her.

"You young bad 'un. You had no business poking around here!"

But he stopped quickly when he saw Dickon pushing the wheelchair behind her.

"Do you know who I am?" demanded Colin.

Ben Weatherstaff was stunned.

"Aye, I do—you are the poor cripple," he said.

"I am not a cripple!" Colin cried out, furiously.

"Don't you have a crooked back?"

"No!" shouted Colin.

Then, as Dickon held his arm, Colin slowly put his feet onto the grass and moved his weight onto his thin legs. For the first time, he stood upright.

Tears ran down Ben Weatherstaff's cheeks.

"Eh!" he said. "The lies folk tell! You'll be a man yet!"

"Get down from the ladder, and Mary will let you in," Colin said. "I want to talk to you."

So Mary opened the door and let Ben inside.

"Please keep our secret," said Colin. "I want to visit the garden as much as I can."

Ben admitted that for years he had come into the secret garden and pruned the roses, because he had been so fond of Colin's mother. But now he was too old to climb over the wall.

"How'd you like to plant a rose? I can get you a rose in a pot," said Ben.

"Go and get it!" said Colin, excitedly.

Dickon took his shovel and helped Colin to dig the hole. Ben brought the rose from the greenhouse.

"Here, lad," he said. "Set it in the ground."

"It's planted!" said Colin, at last, and he looked up at the sky, glowing with happiness.

Dickon's Mother

One evening, Dickon told his mother all about Colin and the secret garden.

"My word!" she said. "It was a good thing that little lass came to the manor. It's been the making of her and it's saved him. What do the folk at the manor make of it all?"

"They don't know," answered Dickon. "Colin has to keep complaining and pretending that he is still unwell, so that they don't guess. If the doctor knew that Colin was recovering, he'd write and tell Mr. Craven, and Colin wants to show his father himself."

Day by day, Colin had begun to eat more. He put on weight and his cheeks gained a healthy glow. One day, Dickon stood on the grass and slowly went through some simple muscle exercises. Colin watched them with widening eyes.

"You must do them gently at first and be careful not to tire yourself. Rest in between times and take deep breaths and don't do too much," said Dickon.

"I'll be careful," said Colin. "Can you show me, please, Dickon?"

Colin could do the exercises while he was sitting down but, after a while, he gently did a few standing on his newly steady feet. Mary began to do them, too.

The secret garden grew more beautiful each day, with flowers in every tiny space.

One morning, Colin was weeding when he stood up and stretched.

"Mary! Dickon!" he called. "Just look at me! I'm well! I shall live forever and ever! I shall find out about people and creatures and everything that grows, just like Dickon. I feel as if I want to shout out something thankful and joyful!"

Just then, the door in the ivy-covered wall opened, and a woman walked in.

"It's Mother!" Dickon cried. "I told her where the door to the secret garden was hidden."

Colin had heard a lot about Mrs. Sowerby, and was delighted that she had come.

"Are you surprised because I am so well?" he asked. She put her hand on his shoulder and wiped the tears away from her eyes.

"Yes, I am," she said. "I knew your mother and you look so much like her that it made my heart jump!"

"Do you think," said Colin, a little awkwardly, "that it will make my father like me?"

"Oh, yes, dear lad," she answered, smiling kindly. They led her around the garden and told her everything they had been doing. Mrs. Sowerby had brought them a picnic, and she sat and watched as they ate it. She was fun and made them laugh. Then they told her how difficult it was to keep pretending that Colin was sick.

"You won't have to keep it up much longer," she said. "Mr. Craven is sure to come home soon."

A Surprise Visit

While the secret garden was coming alive, Archibald Craven was traveling around Europe. He was never happy but, one morning, a feeling of calm crept over him. He had been miserable for ten years, but now he thought of home. He wondered about his son, but was afraid of what he would find if he went back. As the summer passed, he felt stronger —just as Colin did playing outside in the fresh air. Then, one day, he dreamed he heard his wife calling him into the garden. When he woke, there was a letter from Mrs. Sowerby waiting for him. She reminded him that they had met once before on the moor, and that they had spoken about Mary. She said she thought there was now good reason for him to return home.

"I will go back to Misselthwaite at once," he said.

On his journey, he thought about Colin, and wondered whether the boy was dying. In just a few days, he was home. On the drive across the moor to the house he decided to find the buried key to the garden. He had been thinking about all the happy times they had spent there, and wanted to see it again.

But, when he arrived at the manor, Mrs. Medlock told him that Colin was already in the garden. Shocked, Mr. Craven walked to where the thick ivy hung over the door, and heard laughter coming from inside the walls. He heard running feet, and then the door was flung open and a boy ran straight into him.

He was a tall, handsome boy, glowing with life and, when he threw the thick hair back from his forehead, his gray eyes made Mr. Craven gasp.

"Who ... What?" he stammered.

This was not the meeting Colin had planned, but he drew himself up to his very tallest.

"Father," he said, "I'm Colin. You can't believe it, can you? It was the garden that did it, and Mary and Dickon and the animals. We kept it a secret!"

Mr. Craven put his hands on the boy's shoulders and held him still. He dared not speak for a moment.

"Take me into the garden, my boy," he said at last. "And tell me all about it."

The garden was filled with autumn color. Late roses climbed in the sunshine. Mr. Craven looked around him in wonder. They sat down under a tree, all except Colin, who wanted to stand while he told the story.

"So now the garden doesn't need to be a secret any more," Colin said, at last. "And I'm never going to use the wheelchair again."

Ben Weatherstaff had been listening and dashed back to the house to tell the servants what had happened. Mrs. Medlock shrieked with delight when they saw the master of Misselthwaite coming across the lawn, looking happier than they had ever seen him. And, by his side, with his head up in the air, walking strongly and steadily, was Master Colin.

About the Author

Born in Manchester, England, in 1849, Frances Eliza Hodgson was the eldest daughter of a large family. As a young girl she scrawled stories on old sheets of paper because she could not afford proper writing materials. In 1865, the family moved to Tennessee, and Frances began to send her stories to women's magazines. She wrote her first children's book, *Little Lord Fauntleroy*, in 1886 and based the main character on her youngest son. After her eldest son, Lionel, died tragically in 1890, Frances moved to New York, where she wrote her two most famous stories—*A Little Princess* and *The Secret Garden*. She became very eccentric in her old age and died in 1924.

Other titles in the *Illustrated Classics* series:

The Adventures of Tom Sawyer • *Alice's Adventures in Wonderland* • *Anne of Green Gables*
Black Beauty • *Gulliver's Travels* • *Heidi* • *A Little Princess* • *Little Women* • *Pinocchio*
Robin Hood • *Robinson Crusoe* • *The Three Musketeers* • *Treasure Island*
The Wizard of Oz • *20,000 Leagues Under The Sea*

Sandy Creek
NEW YORK

An Imprint of Sterling Publishing
387 Park Avenue South
New York, NY 10016

Text © 2013 by QEB Publishing, Inc.
Illustrations © 2013 by QEB Publishing, Inc.

This 2013 edition published by Sandy Creek.

ISBN 978-1-4351-4819-2

QEB Project Editor: Alexandra Koken • Managing Editor: Victoria Garrard • Design Manager: Anna Lubecka
Editor: Louise John • Designer: Rachel Clark

Manufactured in Guangdong, China
Lot #:
10 9 8 7 6 5 4
06/14